for Stevie

First published 2003 by Walker Books Ltd
87 Vauxhall Walk, London SE11 5HJ

This edition published 2004

4 6 8 10 9 7 5 3

© 2003 Lucy Cousins
Lucy Cousins font © 2003 Lucy Cousins

Maisy™. Maisy is a registered trademark of Walker Books Ltd, London.

The right of Lucy Cousins to be identified as author and illustrator of this work
has been asserted by her in accordance with the Copyright, Designs and Patents Act 1988

Printed in China

British Library Cataloguing in Publication Data:
a catalogue record for this book is available from the British Library

ISBN 1-84428-685-1

www.walkerbooks.co.uk

WALKER BOOKS
AND SUBSIDIARIES
LONDON · BOSTON · SYDNEY · AUCKLAND

Maisy's Rainbow Dream

Lucy Cousins

maisy is fast asleep
in her little bed.
Suddenly a dream begins
inside her head.

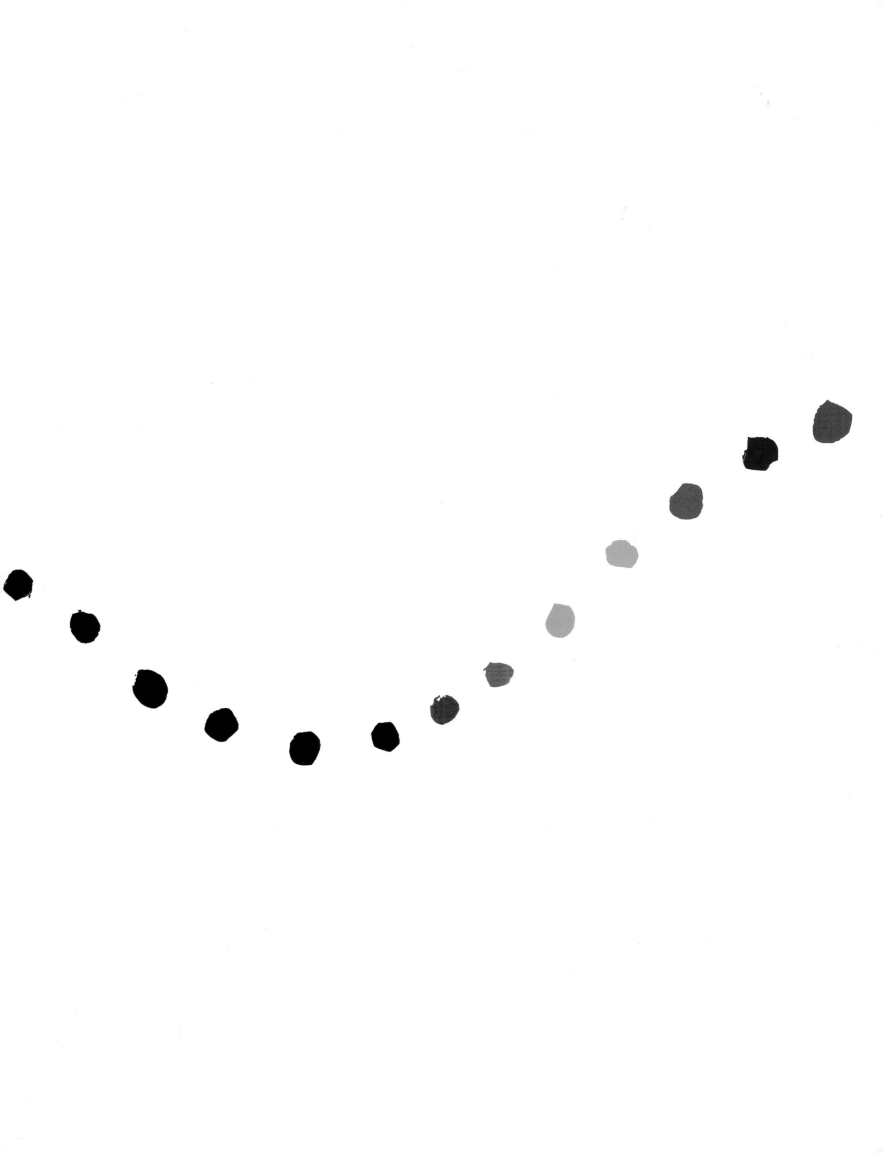

Maisy dreams she is going on a journey. Her friends are coming too.

Maisy dreams
about a
red ladybird.

Maisy dreams about an Orange fish.

maisy dreams about a yellow bee.

Maisy dreams about a green leaf.

Maisy dreams about a blue clock.

maisy dreams about indigo spots.

maisy dreams
about a violet
butterfly.

Maisy dreams she's arrived in Rainbowland.

Wow! It's so

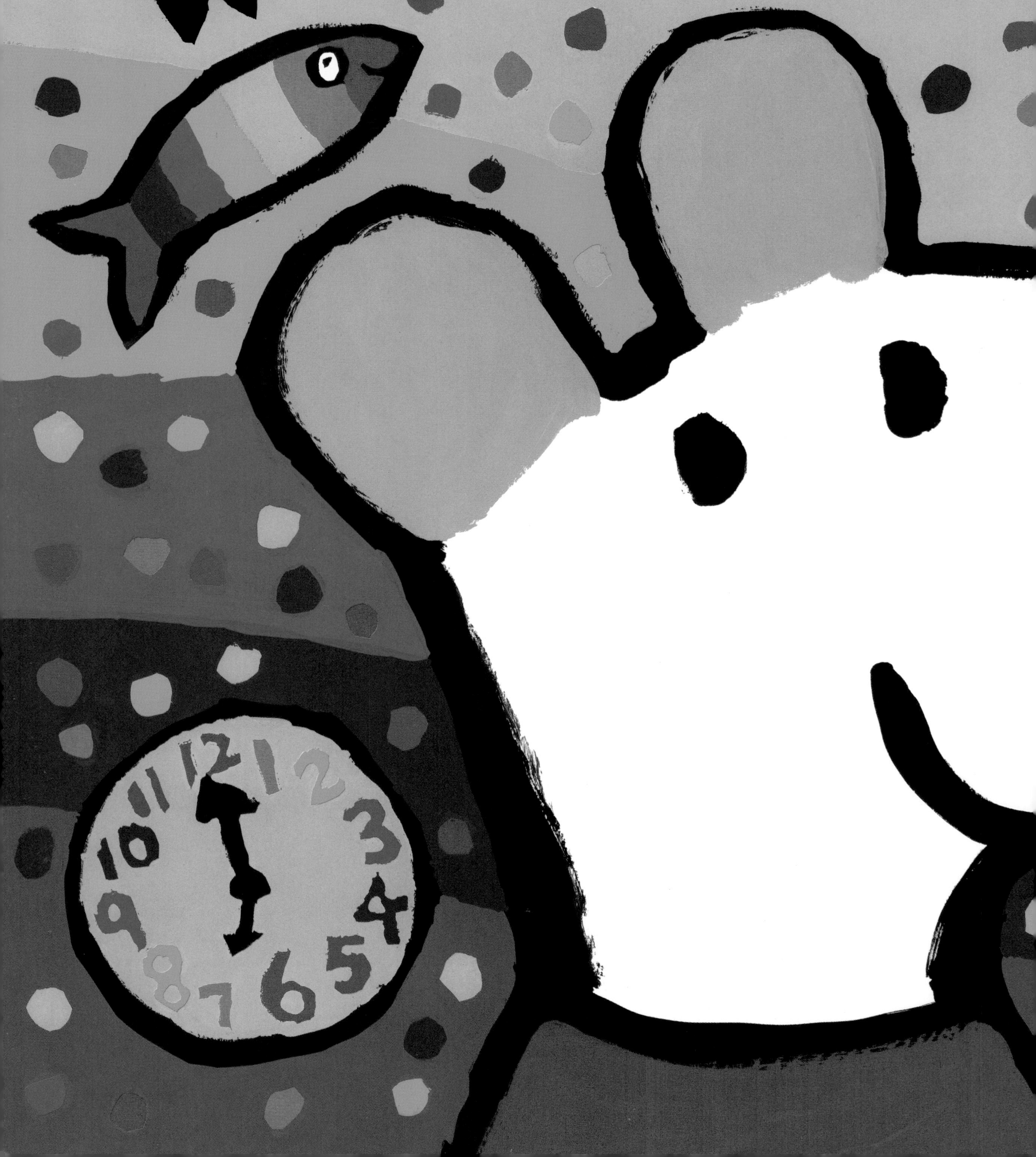

Maisy wakes up from her rainbow dream. Good morning, Maisy. It's a beautiful day!